THE MANSION

By Henry van Dyke

Edited and annotated by Bryson Walker

This edition includes illustrations by Bryson Walker

Walkercrest

Illustrations and book design by Bryson Walker

Published by Walkercrest

Copyright © 2023 by Walkercrest

For more information contact:

publishing@walkercrest.com

www.walkercrest.com

ISBN : 979-8750147410

Second edition : August 2023

Printed in the United States of America.

Foreword

Henry van Dyke wrote The Mansion after having preached sermons for some 30 years and having taught the classics as a literature professor at Princeton. From the "Handbook to the Hymnal" we read, "Dr. Van Dyke's sermons were characterized by great freshness and vitality of style, by beauty of diction, and by breadth of view, as well as by a fearlessness in the declaration of his convictions."

This story is a universal appeal to all of us, no matter what our religious views, to consider our behaviors and our actions in terms of what is really important. Van Dyke invites us to go along with John Weightman who is about to have a profound and miraculous experience that will cause him to rethink his priorities.

CONTENTS

1

THE DIGNIFIED BROWNSTONE MANSION

There was an air of calm and reserved opulence about the Weightman mansion that spoke not of money squandered, but of wealth prudently applied. Standing on a corner of the Avenue no longer fashionable for residence, it looked upon the swelling tide of business with an expression of complacency and half-disdain.

The house was not beautiful. There was nothing in its straight front of chocolate-colored stone, its heavy cornices[1], its broad, staring windows of plate glass, its carved and bronze-bedecked mahogany doors at the top of the wide stoop, to charm the eye or fascinate the imagination. But it was eminently respectable, and in its way imposing.

It seemed to say that the glittering shops of the jewelers, the milliners[2], the confectioners, the florists, the picture-dealers, the furriers[3], the makers of rare and costly antiquities, retail traders in luxuries of life, were beneath the notice of a house that had its foundations in the high finance, and was built literally and figuratively in the shadow of St. Petronius' Church. At the same time there was something self-pleased and congratulatory in the way in which the mansion held its own amid the changing neighborhood. It almost seemed to be lifted up a little, among the tall buildings near at hand, as if it felt the rising value of the land on which it stood.

John Weightman was like the house into which he had built himself thirty years ago, and in which his ideals and ambitions were incrusted. He was a self-made man. But in making himself he had chosen a highly esteemed pattern and worked according to the approved rules. There was nothing irregular, questionable, flamboyant about him. He was solid, correct, and justly successful. His minor tastes, of course, had been carefully kept up to date.

At the proper time, pictures of the Barbizon[4] masters, old English plate and portraits, bronzes by Barye[5] and marbles by Rodin, Persian carpets and Chinese porcelains, had been introduced to the mansion. It contained a Louis Quinze reception-room, an Empire drawing-room, a Jacobean dining-room, and various apartments dimly reminiscent of the styles of furniture affected by deceased monarchs. That the hallways were too short for the historic perspective did not make much difference. American decorative art is capable de tout, it absorbs all periods. Of each period Mr. Weightman wished to have something of the best. He understood its value, present as a certificate, and prospective as an investment. It was only in the architecture of his town house that he remained conservative, immovable, one might almost say Early-Victorian-Christian.

His country house at Dulwich-on-the-Sound was a palace of the Italian Renaissance. But in town he adhered to an architecture which had moral associations, the Nineteenth-Century-Brownstone epoch.

It was a symbol of his social position, his religious doctrine, and even, in a way, of his business creed. "A man of fixed principles," he would say, "should express them in the looks of his house. New York changes its domestic architecture too rapidly. It is like divorce. It is not dignified. I don't like it. Extravagance and fickleness are advertised in most of these new houses. I wish to be known for different qualities. Dignity and prudence are the things that people trust. Everyone knows that I can afford to live in the house that suits me. It is a guarantee to the public. It inspires confidence. It helps my influence. There is a text in the Bible about 'a house that hath foundations.' That is the proper kind of a mansion for a solid man."

Harold Weightman had often listened to his father discoursing in this fashion on the fundamental principles of life, and always with a divided mind. He admired immensely his father's talents and the single-minded energy with which he improved them. But in the paternal philosophy there was something that disquieted and oppressed the young man, and made him gasp inwardly for fresh air and free action.

At times, during his college course and his years at the law school, he had yielded to this impulse and broken away--now toward extravagance and dissipation, and then, when the reaction came, toward a romantic devotion to work among the poor. He had felt his father's disapproval for both of these forms of imprudence; but it was never expressed in a harsh or violent way, always with a certain tolerant patience, such as one might show for the mistakes and vagaries of the very young.

John Weightman was not hasty, impulsive, inconsiderate, even toward his own children. With them, as with the rest of the world, he felt that he had a reputation to maintain, a theory to vindicate. He could afford to give them time to see that he was absolutely right.

One of his favorite Scripture quotations was, "Wait on the Lord." He had applied it to real estate and to people, with profitable results. But to human persons the sensation of being waited for is not always agreeable. Sometimes, especially with the young, it produces a vague restlessness, a dumb resentment, which is increased by the fact that one can hardly explain or justify it. Of this John Weightman was not conscious. It lay beyond his horizon. He did not take it into account in the plan of life which he made for himself and for his family as the sharers and inheritors of his success.

2

THE MAGNIFICENT MRS. WEIGHTMAN

F ather plays us," said Harold to his mother in a voice of disdain, "like a game of chess."

"My dear," said that lady, whose faith in her husband was religious, "you ought not to speak so impatiently. At least he wins the game. He is one of the most respected men in New York. And he is very generous, too."

"I wish he would be more generous in letting us be ourselves," said the young man. "He always has something in view for us and expects to move us up to it."

"But isn't it always for our benefit?" replied his mother. "Look what a position we have. No one can say there is any taint on our money. There are no rumors about your father. He has kept the laws of God and of man. He has never made any mistakes."

Harold got up from his chair and poked the fire. Then he came back to the ample, well-gowned, firm-looking lady, and sat beside her on the sofa. He took her hand gently and looked at the two rings--a thin band of yellow gold, and a small solitaire diamond--which kept their place on her third finger in modest dignity, as if not shamed, but rather justified, by the splendor of the emerald which glittered beside them.

"Mother," he said, "you have a wonderful hand. And father made no mistake when he won you. But are you sure he has always been so inerrant?

"Harold," she exclaimed, a little stiffly, "what do you mean? His life is an open book."

"Oh," he answered, "I don't mean anything bad, mother dear. I know the governor's life is an open book--a ledger, if you like, kept in the best bookkeeping hand, and always ready for inspection--every page correct, and showing a handsome balance. But isn't it a mistake not to allow us to make our own mistakes, to learn for ourselves, to live our own lives? Must we be always working for 'the balance,' in one thing or another? I want to be myself--to get outside of this everlasting, profitable 'plan'--to let myself go, and lose myself for a while at least--to do the things that I want to do, just because I want to do them."

"My boy," said his mother, anxiously, "you are not going to do anything wrong or foolish? You know the falsehood of that old proverb about wild oats."

He threw back his head and laughed. "Yes, mother," he answered, "I know it well enough. But in California, you know, the wild oats are one of the most valuable crops. They grow all over the hillsides and keep the cattle and the horses alive. But that wasn't what I meant--to sow wild oats. Say to pick wild flowers, if you like, or even to chase wild geese--to do something that seems good to me just for its own sake, not for the sake of wages of one kind or another. I feel like a hired man, in the service of this magnificent mansion--say in training for father's place as majordomo[6]. I'd like to get out some way, to feel free--perhaps to do something for others."

The young man's voice hesitated a little. "Yes, it sounds like cant7, I know, but sometimes I feel as if I'd like to do some good in the world, if father only wouldn't insist upon God's putting it into the ledger."

His mother moved uneasily, and a slight look of bewilderment came into her face.

"Isn't that almost irreverent?" she asked. "Surely the righteous must have their reward. And your father is good. See how much he gives to all the established charities, how many things he has founded. He's always thinking of others, and planning for them. And surely, for us, he does everything. How well he has planned this trip to Europe for me and the girls--the court-presentation at Berlin, the season on the Riviera, the visits in England with the Plumptons and the Halverstones. He says Lord Halverstone has the finest old house in Sussex, pure Elizabethan, and all the old customs are kept up, too--family prayers every morning for all the domestics. By-the-way, you know his son Bertie, I believe."

Harold smiled a little to himself as he answered: "Yes, I fished at Catalina Island last June with the Honorable Ethelbert; he's rather a decent chap, in spite of his ingrowing mind. But you?--mother, you are simply magnificent! You are father's masterpiece."

The young man leaned over to kiss her, and went up to the Riding Club for his afternoon canter in the Park.

So it came to pass, early in December, that Mrs. Weightman and her two daughters sailed for Europe, on their serious pleasure trip, even as it had been written in the book of Providence; and John Weightman, who had made the entry, was left to pass the rest of the winter with his son and heir in the brownstone mansion.

They were comfortable enough. The machinery of the massive establishment ran as smoothly as a great electric dynamo. They were busy enough, too. John Weightman's plans and enterprises were complicated, though his principle of action was always simple--to get good value for every expenditure and effort.

The banking-house of which he was the chief, the brain, the will, the absolutely controlling hand, was so admirably organized that the details of its direction took but little time. But the scores of other interests that radiated from it and were dependent upon it--or perhaps it would be more accurate to say, that contributed to its solidity and success--the many investments, industrial, political, benevolent, reformatory, ecclesiastical, that had made the name of Weightman well known and potent in city, church, and state, demanded much attention and careful steering, in order that each might produce the desired result.

There were board meetings of corporations and hospitals, conferences in Wall Street and at Albany[8], consultations and committee meetings in the brownstone mansion.

For a share in all this business and its adjuncts John Weightman had his son in training in one of the famous law firms of the city; for he held that banking itself is a simple affair, the only real difficulties of finance are on its legal side. Meantime he wished the young man to meet and know the men with whom he would have to deal when he became a partner in the house. So a couple of dinners were given in the mansion during December, after which the father called the son's attention to the fact that over a hundred million dollars had sat around the board.

3

A QUARREL ON CHRISTMAS EVE

On Christmas Eve, father and son were dining together without guests, and their talk across the broad table, glittering with silver and cut glass, and softly lit by shaded candles, was intimate, though a little slow at times.

The elder man was in rather a rare mood, more expansive and confidential than usual; and, when the coffee was brought in and they were left alone, he talked more freely of his personal plans and hopes than he had ever done before.

"I feel very grateful tonight," said he, at last; "it must be something in the air of Christmas that gives me this feeling of thankfulness for the many divine mercies that have been bestowed upon me. All the principles by which I have tried to guide my life have been justified. I have never made the value of this salted almond by anything that the courts would not uphold, at least in the long run, and yet--or wouldn't it be truer to say and therefore?--my affairs have been wonderfully prospered. There's a great deal in that text 'Honesty is the best'--but no, that's not from the Bible, after all, is it? Wait a moment; there is something of that kind, I know."

"May I light a cigar, father," said Harold, turning away to hide a smile, "while you are remembering the text?"

"Yes, certainly," answered the elder man, rather shortly; "you know I don't dislike the smell. But it is a wasteful, useless habit, and therefore I have never practised it. Nothing useless is worthwhile, that's my motto--nothing that does not bring the reward. Oh, now I recall the text, 'Verily I say unto you they have their reward.' I shall ask Doctor Snodgrass to preach a sermon on that verse some day."

"Using you as an illustration?"

"Well, not exactly that; but I could give him some good materials from my own experience to prove the truth of Scripture. I can honestly say that there is not one of my charities that has not brought me in a good return, either in the increase of influence, the building up of credit, or the association with substantial people. Of course you have to be careful how you give, in order to secure the best results--no indiscriminate giving--no pennies in beggars' hats! It has been one of my principles always to use the same kind of judgment in charities that I use in my other affairs, and they have not disappointed me."

"Even the check that you put in the plate when you take the offertory up the aisle on Sunday morning?"

"Certainly; though there the influence is less direct; and I must confess that I have my doubts in regard to the collection for Foreign Missions. That always seems to me romantic and wasteful. You never hear from it in any definite way. They say the missionaries have done a good deal to open the way for trade; perhaps--but they have also gotten us into commercial and political difficulties. Yet I give to them--a little--it is a matter of conscience with me to identify myself with all the enterprises of the Church; it is the mainstay of social order and a prosperous civilization. But the best forms of benevolence are the well-established, organized ones here at home, where people can see them and know what they are doing."

"You mean the ones that have a local habitation and a name."

"Yes; they offer by far the safest return, though of course there is something gained by contributing to general funds. A public man can't afford to be without public spirit. But on the whole I prefer a building, or an endowment. There is a mutual advantage to a good name and a good institution in their connection in the public mind. It helps them both. Remember that, my boy. Of course at the beginning you will have to practise it in a small way; later, you will have larger opportunities. But try to put your gifts where they can be identified and do good all around. You'll see the wisdom of it in the long run."

"I can see it already, sir, and the way you describe it looks amazingly wise and prudent. In other words, we must cast our bread on the waters in large loaves, carried by sound ships marked with the owner's name, so that the return freight will be sure to come back to us."

The father laughed, but his eyes were frowning a little as if he suspected something irreverent under the respectful reply.

"You put it humorously, but there's sense in what you say. Why not? God rules the sea; but He expects us to follow the laws of navigation and commerce. Why not take good care of your bread, even when you give it away?"

"It's not for me to say why not--and yet I can think of cases--"

The young man hesitated for a moment. His half-finished cigar had gone out. He rose and tossed it into the fire, in front of which he remained standing--a slender, eager, restless young figure, with a touch of hunger in the fine face, strangely like and unlike the father, at whom he looked with half-wistful curiosity.

"The fact is, sir," he continued, "there is such a case in my mind now, and it is a good deal on my heart, too. So I thought of speaking to you about it tonight. You remember Tom Rollins, the Junior who was so good to me when I entered college?"

The father nodded. He remembered very well indeed the annoying incidents of his son's first escapade, and how Rollins had stood by him and helped to avoid a public disgrace, and how a close friendship had grown between the two boys, so different in their fortunes.

"Yes," he said, "I remember him. He was a promising young man. Has he succeeded?"

"Not exactly--that is not yet. His business has been going rather badly. He has a wife and little baby, you know. And now he has broken down,-- something wrong with his lungs. The doctor says his only chance is a year or eighteen months in Colorado. I wish we could help him."

"How much would it cost?"

"Three or four thousand, perhaps, as a loan."

"Does the doctor say he will get well?"

"A fighting chance--the doctor says."

The face of the older man changed subtly. Not a line was altered, but it seemed to have a different substance, as if it were carved out of some firm, imperishable stuff.

"A fighting chance," he said, "may do for a speculation, but it is not a good investment. You owe something to young Rollins. Your grateful feeling does you credit. But don't overwork it. Send him three or four hundred, if you like. You'll never hear from it again, except in the letter of thanks. But for Heaven's sake don't be sentimental. Religion is not a matter of sentiment; it's a matter of principle."

The face of the younger man changed now. But instead of becoming fixed and graven, it seemed to melt into life by the heat of an inward fire. His nostrils quivered with quick breath, his lips were curled.

"Principle!" he said. "You mean principal--and interest too. Well, sir, you know best whether that is religion or not. But if it is, count me out, please. Tom saved me from going to the devil, six years ago; and I'll be damned if I don't help him to the best of my ability now."

John Weightman looked at his son steadily.

"Harold," he said at last, "you know I dislike violent language, and it never has any influence with me. If I could honestly approve of this proposition of yours, I'd let you have the money; but I can't; it's extravagant and useless. But you have your Christmas check for a thousand dollars coming to you tomorrow. You can use it as you please. I never interfere with your private affairs."

"Thank you," said Harold. "Thank you very much! But there's another private affair. I want to get away from this life, this town, this house. It stifles me. You refused last summer when I asked you to let me go up to Grenfell's Mission on the Labrador. I could go now, at least as far as the Newfoundland Station. Have you changed your mind?"

"Not at all. I think it is an exceedingly foolish enterprise. It would interrupt the career that I have marked out for you."

"Well, then, here's a cheaper proposition. Algy Vanderhoof wants me to join him on his yacht with--well, with a little party--to cruise in the West Indies. Would you prefer that?"

"Certainly not! The Vanderhoof set is wild and godless--I do not wish to see you keeping company with fools who walk in the broad and easy way that leads to perdition."

"It is rather a hard choice," said the young man, with a short laugh, turning toward the door. "According to you there's very little difference--a fool's paradise or a fool's hell! Well, it's one or the other for me, and I'll toss up for it tonight: heads, I lose; tails, the devil wins. Anyway, I'm sick of this, and I'm out of it."

"Harold," said the older man (and there was a slight tremor in his voice), "don't let us quarrel on Christmas Eve. All I want is to persuade you to think seriously of the duties and responsibilities to which God has called you--don't speak lightly of heaven and hell--remember, there is another life."

The young man came back and laid his hand upon his father's shoulder.

"Father," he said, "I want to remember it. I try to believe in it. But somehow or other, in this house, it all seems unreal to me. No doubt all you say is perfectly right and wise. I don't venture to argue against it, but I can't feel it--that's all. If I'm to have a soul, either to lose or to save, I must really live. Just now neither the present nor the future means anything to me. But surely we won't quarrel. I'm very grateful to you, and we'll part friends. Good-night, sir."

The father held out his hand in silence. The heavy portiere dropped noiselessly behind the son, and he went up the wide, curving stairway to his own room.

Meantime John Weightman sat in his carved chair in the Jacobean dining room. He felt strangely old and dull. The portraits of beautiful women by Lawrence and Reynolds and Raeburn, which had often seemed like real company to him, looked remote and uninteresting. He fancied something cold and almost unfriendly in their expression, as if they were staring through him or beyond him. They cared nothing for his principles, his hopes, his disappointments, his successes; they belonged to another world, in which he had no place. At this he felt a vague resentment, a sense of discomfort that he could not have defined or explained. He was used to being considered, respected, appreciated at his full value in every region, even in that of his own dreams.

4

A LAND STRANGE AND WONDERFUL

P resently, John Weightman rang for the butler, telling him to close the house and not to sit up, and walked with lagging steps into the long library, where the shaded lamps were burning.

His eye fell upon the low shelves full of costly books, but he had no desire to open them. Even the carefully chosen pictures that hung above them seemed to have lost their attraction. He paused for a moment before an idyll of Corot--a dance of nymphs around some forgotten altar in a vaporous glade--and looked at it curiously. There was something rapturous and serene about the picture, a breath of spring-time in the misty trees, a harmony of joy in the dancing figures, that wakened in him a feeling of half-pleasure and half-envy. It represented something that he had never known in his calculated, orderly life. He was dimly mistrustful of it.

"It is certainly very beautiful," he thought, "but it is distinctly pagan; that altar is built to some heathen god. It does not fit into the scheme of a Christian life. I doubt whether it is consistent with the tone of my house. I will sell it this winter. It will bring three or four times what I paid for it. That was a good purchase, a very good bargain."

He dropped into the revolving chair before his big library table. It was covered with pamphlets and reports of the various enterprises in which he was interested. There was a pile of newspaper clippings in which his name was mentioned with praise for his sustaining power as a pillar of finance, for his judicious benevolence, for his support of wise and prudent reform movements, for his discretion in making permanent public gifts--"the Weightman Charities," one very complacent editor called them, as if they deserved classification as a distinct species.

He turned the papers over listlessly. There was a description and a picture of the "Weightman Wing of the Hospital for Cripples," of which he was president; and an article on the new professor in the "Weightman Chair of Political Jurisprudence" in Jackson University, of which he was a trustee; and an illustrated account of the opening of the "Weightman Grammar-School" at Dulwich-on-the-Sound, where he had his legal residence for purposes of taxation. This last was perhaps the most carefully planned of all the Weightman Charities. He desired to win the confidence and support of his rural neighbors. It had pleased him much when the local newspaper had spoken of him as an ideal citizen and the logical candidate for the Governorship of the State; but upon the whole it seemed to him wiser to keep out of active politics. It would be easier and better to put Harold into the running, to have him sent to the Legislature from the Dulwich district, then to the national House, then to the Senate. Why not? The Weightman interests were large enough to need a direct representative and guardian at Washington.

But tonight all these plans came back to him with dust upon them. They were dry and crumbling like forsaken habitations. The son upon whom his complacent ambition had rested had turned his back upon the mansion of his father's hopes. The break might not be final; and in any event there would be much to live for; the fortunes of the family would be secure. But the zest of it all would be gone if John Weightman had to give up the assurance of perpetuating his name and his principles in his son. It was a bitter disappointment, and he felt that he had not deserved it.

He rose from the chair and paced the room with leaden feet. For the first time in his life his age was visibly upon him. His head was heavy and hot, and the thoughts that rolled in it were confused and depressing. Could it be that he had made a mistake in the principles of his existence? There was no argument in what Harold had said--it was almost childish-- and yet it had shaken the elder man more deeply than he cared to show. It held a silent attack which touched him more than open criticism. Suppose the end of his life were nearer than he thought--the end must come some time--what if it were now? Had he not founded his house upon a rock? Had he not kept the Commandments? Was he not, "touching the law, blameless"? And beyond this, even if there were some faults in his character--and all men are sinners-- yet he surely believed in the saving doctrines of religion--the forgiveness of sins, the resurrection of the body, the life everlasting. Yes, that was the true source of comfort, after all. He would read a bit in the Bible, as he did every night, and go to bed and to sleep.

He went back to his chair at the library table. A strange weight of weariness rested upon him, but he opened the book at a familiar place, and his eyes fell upon the verse at the bottom of the page. "Lay not up for yourselves treasures upon earth." That had been the text of the sermon a few weeks before.

Sleepily, heavily, he tried to fix his mind upon it and recall it. What was it that Doctor Snodgrass had said? Ah, yes--that it was a mistake to pause here in reading the verse. We must read on without a pause--Lay not up treasures upon earth where moth and rust do corrupt and where thieves break through and steal--that was the true doctrine. We may have treasures upon earth, but they must not be put into unsafe places, but into safe places. A most comforting doctrine! He had always followed it. Moths and rust and thieves had done no harm to his investments. John Weightman's drooping eyes turned to the next verse, at the top of the second column. "But lay up for yourselves treasures in heaven." Now what had the Doctor said about that? How was it to be understood--in what sense--treasures--in heaven?

The book seemed to float away from him. The light vanished. He wondered dimly if this could be Death, coming so suddenly, so quietly, so irresistibly. He struggled for a moment to hold himself up, and then sank slowly forward upon the table. His head rested upon his folded hands.

He slipped into the unknown. How long afterward conscious life returned to him he did not know. The blank might have been an hour or a century. He knew only that something had happened in the interval. What it was he could not tell. He found great difficulty in catching the thread of his identity again. He felt that he was himself; but the trouble was to make his connections, to verify and place himself, to know who and where he was. At last it grew clear. John Weightman was sitting on a stone, not far from a road in a strange land.

The road was not a formal highway, fenced and graded. It was more like a great travel-trace, worn by thousands of feet passing across the open country in the same direction. Down in the valley, into which he could look, the road seemed to form itself gradually out of many minor paths; little footways coming across the meadows, winding tracks following along beside the streams, faintly marked trails emerging from the woodlands. But on the hillside the threads were more firmly woven into one clear band of travel, though there were still a few dim paths joining it here and there, as if persons had been climbing up the hill by other ways and had turned at last to seek the road.

From the edge of the hill, where John Weightman sat, he could see the travelers, in little groups or larger companies, gathering from time to time by the different paths, and making the ascent. They were all clothed in white, and the form of their garments was strange to him; it was like some old picture. They passed him, group after group, talking quietly together or singing; not moving in haste, but with a certain air of eagerness and joy as if they were glad to be on their way to an appointed place.

They did not stay to speak to him, but they looked at him often and spoke to one another as they looked; and now and then one of them would smile and beckon him a friendly greeting, so that he felt they would like him to be with them.

There was quite an interval between the groups; and he followed each of them with his eyes after it had passed, blanching the long ribbon of the road for a little transient space, rising and receding across the wide, billowy upland, among the rounded hillocks of aerial green and gold and lilac, until it came to the high horizon, and stood outlined for a moment, a tiny cloud of whiteness against the tender blue, before it vanished over the hill.

5

FELLOW TRAVELERS

F or a long time John Weightman sat there watching and wondering. It was a very different world from that in which his mansion on the Avenue was built; and it looked strange to him, but most real--as real as anything he had ever seen.

Presently he felt a strong desire to know what country it was and where the people were going. He had a faint premonition of what it must be, but he wished to be sure. So he rose from the stone where he was sitting, and came down through the short grass and the lavender flowers, toward a passing group of people. One of them turned to meet him, and held out his hand. It was an old man, under whose white beard and brows John Weightman thought he saw a suggestion of the face of the village doctor who had cared for him years ago, when he was a boy in the country.

"Welcome," said the old man. "Will you come with us?"

"Where are you going?"

"To the heavenly city, to see our mansions there."

"And who are these with you?"

"Strangers to me, until a little while ago; I know them better now. But you I have known for a long time, John Weightman. Don't you remember your old doctor?"

"Yes," he cried--"yes; your voice has not changed at all. I'm glad indeed to see you, Doctor McLean, especially now. All this seems very strange to me, almost oppressive. I wonder if-- but may I go with you, do you suppose?"

"Surely," answered the doctor, with his familiar smile; "it will do you good. And you also must have a mansion in the city waiting for you--a fine one, too--are you not looking forward to it?"

"Yes," replied the other, hesitating a moment; "yes--I believe it must be so, although I had not expected to see it so soon. But I will go with you, and we can talk by the way."

The two men quickly caught up with the other people, and all went forward together along the road. The doctor had little to tell of his experience, for it had been a plain, hard life, uneventfully spent for others, and the story of the village was very simple.

John Weightman's adventures and triumphs would have made a far richer, more imposing history, full of contacts with the great events and personages of the time. But somehow or other he did not care to speak much about it, walking on that wide heavenly moorland, under that tranquil, sunless arch of blue, in that free air of perfect peace, where the light was diffused without a shadow, as if the spirit of life in all things were luminous.

There was only one person besides the doctor in that little company whom John Weightman had known before--an old bookkeeper who had spent his life over a desk, carefully keeping accounts--a rusty, dull little man, patient and narrow, whose wife had been in the insane asylum for twenty years and whose only child was a crippled daughter, for whose comfort and happiness he had toiled and sacrificed himself without stint. It was a surprise to find him here, as care-free and joyful as the rest.

The lives of others in the company were revealed in brief glimpses as they talked together--a mother, early widowed, who had kept her little flock of children together and labored through hard and heavy years to bring them up in purity and knowledge--a Sister of Charity who had devoted herself to the nursing of poor folk who were being eaten to death by cancer--a schoolmaster whose heart and life had been poured into his quiet work of training boys for a clean and thoughtful manhood--a medical missionary who had given up a brilliant career in science to take the charge of a hospital in darkest Africa--a beautiful woman with silver hair who had resigned her dreams of love and marriage to care for an invalid father, and after his death had made her life a long, steady search for ways of doing kindnesses to others--a poet who had walked among the crowded tenements of the great city, bringing cheer and comfort not only by his songs, but by his wise and patient works of practical aid--a paralyzed woman who had lain for thirty years upon her bed, helpless but not hopeless, succeeding by a miracle of courage in her single aim, never to complain, but always to impart a bit of joy and peace to everyone who came near her.

All these, and other persons like them, people of little consideration in the world, but now seemingly all full of great contentment and an inward gladness that made their steps light, were in the company that passed along the road, talking together of things past and things to come, and singing now and then with clear voices from which the veil of age and sorrow was lifted. John Weightman joined in some of the songs--which were familiar to him from their use in the church--at first with a touch of hesitation, and then more confidently. For as they went on his sense of strangeness and fear at his new experience diminished, and his thoughts began to take on their habitual assurance and complacency. Were not these people going to the Celestial City? And was not he in his right place among them?

He had always looked forward to this journey. If they were sure, each one, of finding a mansion there, could not he be far more sure? His life had been more fruitful than theirs. He had been a leader, a founder of new enterprises, a pillar of Church and State, a prince of the House of Israel.

Ten talents had been given him, and he had made them twenty. His reward would be proportionate. He was glad that his companions were going to find fit dwellings prepared for them; but he thought also with a certain pleasure of the surprise that some of them would feel when they saw his appointed mansion.

6

MANY MANSIONS

They came to the summit of the moorland and looked over into the world beyond. It was a vast, green plain, softly rounded like a shallow vase, and circled with hills of amethyst. A broad, shining river flowed through it, and many silver threads of water were woven across the green; and there were borders of tall trees on the banks of the river, and orchards full of roses abloom along the little streams, and in the midst of all stood the city, white and wonderful and radiant. When the travelers saw it they were filled with awe and joy.

They passed over the little streams and among the orchards quickly and silently, as if they feared to speak lest the city should vanish. The wall of the city was very low, a child could see over it, for it was made only of precious stones, which are never large.

The gate of the city was not like a gate at all, for it was not barred with iron or wood, but only a single pearl, softly gleaming, marked the place where the wall ended and the entrance lay open. A person stood there whose face was bright and grave, and whose robe was like the flower of the lily, not a woven fabric, but a living texture.

"Come in," he said to the company of travelers; "you are at your journey's end, and your mansions are ready for you."

John Weightman hesitated, for he was troubled by a doubt. Suppose that he was not really, like his companions, at his journey's end, but only transported for a little while out of the regular course of his life into this mysterious experience? Suppose that, after all, he had not really passed through the door of death, like these others, but only through the door of dreams, and was walking in a vision, a living man among the blessed dead. Would it be right for him to go with them into the heavenly city? Would it not be a deception, a desecration, a deep and unforgivable offense?

The strange, confusing question had no reason in it, as he very well knew; for if he was dreaming, then it was all a dream; but if his companions were real, then he also was with them in reality, and if they had died then he must have died too. Yet he could not rid his mind of the sense that there was a difference between them and him, and it made him afraid to go on. But, as he paused and turned, the Keeper of the Gate looked straight and deep into his eyes, and beckoned to him. Then he knew that it was not only right but necessary that he should enter.

They passed from street to street among fair and spacious dwellings, set in amaranthine gardens, and adorned with an infinitely varied beauty of divine simplicity. The mansions differed in size, in shape, in charm: each one seemed to have its own personal look of loveliness; yet all were alike in fitness to their place, in harmony with one another, in the addition which each made to the singular and tranquil splendor of the city.

As the little company came, one by one, to the mansions which were prepared for them, and their Guide beckoned to the happy inhabitant to enter in and take possession, there was a soft murmur of joy, half wonder and half recognition; as if the new and immortal dwelling were crowned with the beauty of surprise, lovelier and nobler than all the dreams of it had been; and yet also as if it were touched with the beauty of the familiar, the remembered, the long-loved.

One after another the travelers were led to their own mansions, and went in gladly; and from within, through the open doorways came sweet voices of welcome, and low laughter, and song. At last there was no one left with the Guide but the two old friends, Doctor McLean and John Weightman. They were standing in front of one of the largest and fairest of the houses, whose garden glowed softly with radiant flowers.

The Guide laid his hand upon the doctor's shoulder. "This is for you," he said. "Go in; there is no more pain here, no more death, nor sorrow, nor tears; for your old enemies are all conquered. But all the good that you have done for others, all the help that you have given, all the comfort that you have brought, all the strength and love that you have bestowed upon the suffering, are here; for we have built them all into this mansion for you."

The good man's face was lighted with a still joy. He clasped his old friend's hand closely, and whispered: "How wonderful it is! Go on, you will come to your mansion next, it is not far away, and we shall see each other again soon, very soon."

So he went through the garden, and into the music within. The Keeper of the Gate turned to John Weightman with level, quiet, searching eyes. Then he asked, gravely: "Where do you wish me to lead you now?"

"To see my own mansion," answered the man, with half-concealed excitement. "Is there not one here for me? You may not let me enter it yet, perhaps, for I must confess to you that I am only--"

"I know," said the Keeper of the Gate--"I know it all. You are John Weightman."

"Yes," said the man, more firmly than he had spoken at first, for it gratified him that his name was known.

"Yes, I am John Weightman, Senior Warden of St. Petronius' Church. I wish very much to see my mansion here, if only for a moment. I believe that you have one for me. Will you take me to it?"

The Keeper of the Gate drew a little book from the breast of his robe and turned over the pages. "Certainly," he said, with a curious look at the man, "your name is here; and you shall see your mansion if you will follow me." It seemed as if they must have walked miles and miles, through the vast city, passing street after street of houses larger and smaller, of gardens richer and poorer, but all full of beauty and delight. They came into a kind of suburb, where there were many small cottages, with plots of flowers, very lowly, but bright and fragrant.

7

THIS IS YOUR MANSION

F inally they reached an open field, bare and lonely-looking. There were two or three little bushes in it, without flowers, and the grass was sparse and thin.

In the center of the field was a tiny hut, hardly big enough for a shepherd's shelter. It looked as if it had been built of discarded things, scraps and fragments of other buildings, put together with care and pains, by someone who had tried to make the most of cast-off material.

There was something pitiful and shamefaced about the hut. It shrank and drooped and faded in its barren field, and seemed to cling only by sufferance to the edge of the splendid city.

"This," said the Keeper of the Gate, standing still and speaking with a low, distinct voice--"this is your mansion, John Weightman."

An almost intolerable shock of grieved wonder and indignation choked the man for a moment so that he could not say a word. Then he turned his face away from the poor little hut and began to remonstrate eagerly with his companion.

"Surely, sir," he stammered, "you must be in error about this. There is something wrong--some other John Weightman--a confusion of names--the book must be mistaken."

"There is no mistake," said the Keeper of the Gate, very calmly; "here is your name, the record of your title and your possessions in this place."

"But how could such a house be prepared for me," cried the man, with a resentful tremor in his voice--"for me, after my long and faithful service? Is this a suitable mansion for one so well known and devoted? Why is it so pitifully small and mean? Why have you not built it large and fair, like the others?"

"That is all the material you sent us."

"What!"

"We have used all the material that you sent us," repeated the Keeper of the Gate.

"Now I know that you are mistaken," cried the man, with growing earnestness, "for all my life long I have been doing things that must have supplied you with material. Have you not heard that I have built a school-house; the wing of a hospital; two--yes, three--small churches, and the greater part of a large one, the spire of St. Petro--"

The Keeper of the Gate lifted his hand. "Wait," he said; "we know all these things. They were not ill done. But they were all marked and used as foundation for the name and mansion of John Weightman in the world. Did you not plan them for that?"

"Yes," answered the man, confused and taken aback, "I confess that I thought often of them in that way. Perhaps my heart was set upon that too much. But there are other things--my endowment for the college--my steady and liberal contributions to all the established charities--my support of every respectable--"

"Wait," said the Keeper of the Gate again. "Were not all these carefully recorded on earth where they would add to your credit? They were not foolishly done. Verily, you have had your reward for them. Would you be paid twice?"

"No," cried the man, with deepening dismay, "I dare not claim that. I acknowledge that I considered my own interest too much. But surely not altogether. You have said that these things were not foolishly done. They accomplished some good in the world. Does not that count for something?"

"Yes," answered the Keeper of the Gate, "it counts in the world--where you counted it. But it does not belong to you here. We have saved and used everything that you sent us. This is the mansion prepared for you."

As he spoke, his look grew deeper and more searching, like a flame of fire. John Weightman could not endure it. It seemed to strip him naked and wither him. He sank to the ground under a crushing weight of shame, covering his eyes with his hands and cowering face downward upon the stones. Dimly through the trouble of his mind he felt their hardness and coldness.

"Tell me, then," he cried, brokenly, "since my life has been so little worth, how came I here at all?"

"Through the mercy of the King"--the answer was like the soft tolling of a bell.

"And how have I earned it?" he murmured.

"It is never earned; it is only given," came the clear, low reply.

"But how have I failed so wretchedly," he asked, "in all the purpose of my life? What could I have done better? What is it that counts here?"

"Only that which is truly given," answered the bell-like voice. Only that good which is done for the love of doing it. Only those plans in which the welfare of others is the master thought. Only those labors in which the sacrifice is greater than the reward. Only those gifts in which the giver forgets himself."

The man lay silent. A great weakness, an unspeakable despondency and humiliation were upon him. But the face of the Keeper of the Gate was infinitely tender as he bent over him.

"Think again, John Weightman. Has there been nothing like that in your life?"

"Nothing," he sighed. "If there ever were such things, it must have been long ago--they were all crowded out--I have forgotten them."

There was an ineffable smile on the face of the Keeper of the Gate, and his hand made the sign of the cross over the bowed head as he spoke gently: "These are the things that the King never forgets; and because there were a few of them in your life, you have a little place here."

The sense of coldness and hardness under John Weightman's hands grew sharper and more distinct. The feeling of bodily weariness and lassitude weighed upon him, but there was a calm, almost a lightness, in his heart as he listened to the fading vibrations of the silvery bell-tones.

The chimney clock on the mantel had just ended the last stroke of seven as he lifted his head from the table. Thin, pale strips of the city morning were falling into the room through the narrow partings of the heavy curtains. What was it that had happened to him? Had he been ill? Had he died and come to life again? Or had he only slept, and had his soul had gone visiting in dreams?

8

A CHANGED HEART

J ohn Weightman sat for some time, motionless, not lost, but finding himself in thought. Then he took a narrow book from the table drawer, wrote a check, and tore it out.

He went slowly up the stairs, knocked very softly at his son's door, and, hearing no answer, entered without noise.

Harold was asleep, his bare arm thrown above his head, and his eager face relaxed in peace.

His father looked at him a moment with strangely shining eyes, and then tiptoed quietly to the writing-desk, found a pencil and a sheet of paper, and wrote rapidly: "My dear boy, here is what you asked me for; do what you like with it, and ask for more if you need it. If you are still thinking of that work with Grenfell, we'll talk it over today after church. I want to know your heart better; and if I have made mistakes-"

A slight noise made him turn his head. Harold was sitting up in bed with wide-open eyes. "

"Father!" he cried, "is that you?"

"Yes, my son," answered John Weightman; "I've come back--I mean I've come up--no, I mean come in--well, here I am, and may God give us a good Christmas together."

The End

About the Author

Henry Van Dyke was born on November 10, 1852, in Germantown, Pennsylvania in the United States. Being the son of a clergyman, Henry grew up with an interest in religion. He received a bachelor's degree from Princeton University in 1873 and a master's degree in 1876, followed by a divinity degree from Princeton Seminary in 1877, then additional education at the University of Berlin. Van Dyke served as a professor of English literature at Princeton between 1899 and 1923.

The Mansion was written when Henry van Dyke was about 57 years old and was both a professor of English literature at Princeton and a pastor at the Brick Presbyterian Church in New York City. When one also takes into account that he was a devoted family man with a wife and nine children, it is hard to believe that he found any time to write at all. Yet, he authored over seventy books, contributed to thirty others, and published more than 20 smaller pamphlets, several hymns and dozens of written sermons.

President Woodrow Wilson, a friend and former classmate of van Dyke, appointed him to be an ambassador to the Netherlands and Luxembourg in 1913. World War I broke out and Americans all around Europe rushed to Holland as a place of refuge. Although he had little experience as an ambassador, van Dyke conducted himself with the skill of a trained diplomat. He fought for the rights and safety of Americans throughout Europe and organized efforts for their relief.

When Van Dyke returned to America, he became a friend of Helen Keller. Keller wrote: "Dr. van Dyke is the kind of a friend to have when one is up against a difficult problem. He will take trouble, days and nights of trouble, if it is for somebody else or for some cause he is interested in."

Van Dyke's personal papers are filled with correspondence with literary, religious, and political leaders of his day.

Dr. Henry van Dyke died in April 1933 at the age of 80 and was buried in the Princeton Cemetery.

"I'm not an optimist, there's too much evil in the world and in me.

Nor am I a pessimist; there is too much good in the world and in God.

So I am just a meliorist, believing that He wills to make the world better, and trying to do my bit to help and wishing that it were more."

Glossary

1. Cornices: A strip of decorative wood usually fitted at the corner where the wall meets the ceiling of a room
2. Milliner: a person or shop who makes or sells women's hats.
3. Furrier: a person or shop who sells furs
4. Barbizon masters: A group of painters who studied together in the village of Barbizon, France from 1830 to 1870 and produced realistic paintings of landscapes.
5. Antoine Louis Barye (French, 1796 ~ 1875) Barye was a French sculptor most famous for his work in depicting wild animals
6. Majordomo: The head administrator of a large household
7. Cant: To boast of your own religious values
8. Albany: The capital city of the state of New York

There is an eBook version and an audiobook dramatization of this story available from Walkercrest.

Thank you for your patronage.

Walkercrest

Made in United States
Orlando, FL
15 December 2023

41079902R00036